The Missing Girl

The Missing Girl

Jacqueline Doyle

Black
Lawrence
Press

Black
Lawrence
Press
www.blacklawrence.com

Executive Editor: Diane Goettel
Chapbook Editor: Kit Frick
Book and Cover Design: Amy Freels
Cover Art: "Inhospitable" by Raeleen Kao. Used with permission.

ISBN: 978-1-62557-983-6

Published 2017 by Black Lawrence Press.
Printed in the United States.

for the missing girls

The dark spot by the road that you might not notice at all is, you see, the beginning of everything. There is a clump of elders there as used to grow beside the road before our house back in Winesburg, Ohio, and in among the elders there is something hidden. It is a woman, that's what it is.

—Sherwood Anderson, *Winesburg, Ohio*

No missing child is ever forgotten, no matter how long they have been missing.

—National Center for Missing and Exploited Children

Contents

The Missing Girl

You see her posters on telephone poles all over town. EULA JOHNSON, MISSING. Some have been torn down, only the stapled corners remaining. Others are blurred and warped from rain.

In the black and white photo, not much bigger than a thumbprint, her limp blonde hair falls to her shoulders. She's wearing a white blouse buttoned to her chin, and she's smiling at the camera. A tentative smile, like maybe she knew something was going to happen. Or like she was used to wanting things she knew she wasn't going to get.

Date of Birth: August 14, 1997

Place of Birth: Fresno, California

Height: 5'0"

Weight: 111 pounds

Hair: Blonde

Eyes: Blue-Gray

Race: Caucasian

Wearing: Blue jeans, green t-shirt, maroon windbreaker

Last seen walking alone on Jerrold Road in Modesto, California at 4:00 p.m. on Wednesday, November 17, 2011. If you have any information concerning this person, please contact the San Joaquin County Sheriff's tip line at 1-209-958-4826, or call your local FBI office.

You can see her in your mind's eye, perky smile dimming, fear dawning in her eyes. Yes, you feel like you know this girl. Just the kind to go missing. Awkward and shy. Inexperienced and eager. Tender, playing brave. Dirt poor. You know. The kind of girl who'll step right into your car if you call her pretty.

Him you're not so sure of. Cowboy hat and a Silverado pickup? Baseball cap and a Mustang? Or a Tahoe maybe, black and sprayed with mud. You can't see his face. He could be anyone, after all. But you can feel the tingle in his groin when he saw her, how his breath must have quickened. You drive this way a lot, wondering where he picked her up, where he took her, what he did, whether she liked it. Eula Johnson.

Jerrold Road is empty today. Birds gather in one of the tall, bare trees by the roadside, jabbering. Dead leaves whirl in the wake of a chilly gust of wind. Yellow grass. Gray sky. Not a car in sight. Just a girl in a gray sweatshirt, hood up against the cold, walking.

Slow way down and hit the button for the passenger window.

Go ahead, say it. "Hey, pretty girl. Want a lift?"

And as she buckles her seat belt (after all, she's not a reckless girl), "So what's your name, sweetheart?"

"Early. Early Halliday."

"I'm Late," you say, sniggering a little. "Guess you probably heard that one before."

She tucks a pale strand of hair behind her ear and looks down at her lap. Her skin is very white, almost translucent. You can see a tracing of light blue veins in her neck.

"I just bet a lot of boys have called you pretty, Early."

Watch her blush as she turns wondering eyes to you. Take your foot off the brake pedal and step on the accelerator. Don't speed. You'll want to take this slow.

You Never Know

"Thank God for small blessings," the woman in the seat next to me repeats. "All I can say is thank God. You never know, do you? You just never know."

"Here's your complimentary club soda, sir, and your peanuts. That will be seven dollars for the Jack Daniel's." I hand my card to the stewardess, reaching over my seatmate, who's absorbed in the story she's telling me and doesn't seem to notice.

She's stagy-looking, with heavy mascara and an oversized purple scarf flung over her left shoulder. In her forties maybe, made up to look younger, wearing an ample black dress designed to camouflage her weight. I wonder if she's a small-time actress. She's flirtatious, not my type at all. She's drinking a Bloody Mary out of a plastic cup and has been talking for twenty minutes.

"The train I missed was the one that crashed," she says in a hushed voice. "I could have died. I mean it could have been me on that train. I could have been one of the ones who died, you know? Or one of the survivors who lived to tell the tale, like right now, sitting next to you on this plane."

I nod politely and sip my scotch and soda. I'm having trouble opening the packet of peanuts. There's a slit on the top, but I can't seem to tear it, and then I do, and the peanuts rain onto the tray table in front of me.

"It was close. I took a train just three days before the one that crashed. It was the morning train and not the afternoon one, but still, close enough, you know. I mean it makes you think. It would make anyone think. Did you see it on the news? All those people wandering around shell-shocked in the debris and smoke. Paramedics rushing around with stretchers. I was almost there. It just gives me the shivers."

She puts her hand up to her throat and shakes her head. Her nails are manicured and painted dark maroon.

"But you weren't there." I'm sure I could tell a story with more point than hers. It's annoying, all her dramatics over nothing. She reminds me of my first wife, who was always emoting.

"Close enough. It's like I could feel the wings of the angel of death brushing me. Have you ever had that feeling?"

"As a matter of fact, I have."

"Really?" She puts down her drink and turns to inspect me.

"It was in a car, not a train."

She's nodding, like she knows what I'm going to say.

"I was driving on Route 80 late at night. It was snowing. You could see flurries in the headlights maybe three feet in front of the car, but that's all. Otherwise it was pitch dark. Not a soul in the universe, just me in the car. Or that's the way it felt."

Mascara flecks the pancake makeup under her eyes. Her face can't be more than a foot away from mine.

I'm not sure where I'm going with this, or why. Generally I'm a listener, not a storyteller. And I'd describe myself as honest to a fault. I lie once in a while to my wife, but they're white lies, to preserve domestic harmony. "This is only my second drink." "No, those jeans don't make you look fat." "I missed you too. It's hell, having to travel so much." The same lies everyone tells when there's no point in telling the truth.

I take a long sip of my drink.

"This was a long time ago. I was driving this old beater, and the tires were pretty worn. I was worried about sliding off the road, and I was playing the accelerator, trying to keep my foot off the brake. I can't remember where I was. Ohio maybe. It was a long stretch with no human beings in sight. No buildings. No lights. That's all I remember."

"I'm from Southern California. Would you believe I've never once driven in snow? I would've just died." She puts her hand on her chest as if to calm her fluttering heart. "You know a friend of mine was in a ten-car pileup near Tahoe. She said . . ."

I interrupt. "It was a challenge all right, and I think I'm a pretty good driver, always in control. I would have stopped, but there was nowhere to stop. I remember the windshield wipers were going, and I was just creeping along, trying to see. What I wouldn't have done for an all-night diner, or a motel. I was looking for a motel, I remember that."

I can see the windshield fogging up, the heavy, white clumps of snow pushed aside as the wipers move rhythmically back and forth, feel my foot hovering over the gas pedal.

"I thought about pulling over to see if the snow would let up, but it was too cold to turn the engine off, and I knew I'd run out of gas if I left it running. So I was stuck, inching along, this kid whining in the seat next to me."

Her eyes widen. "So you weren't alone?"

"I guess not." I don't know where this detail came from. Once you start lying, you don't know what's going to come out.

"She just wouldn't shut up, and I was trying to see the road, keep us from landing in the ditch."

"Was it your daughter?"

"No, my wife and I don't have kids. Anyway, it doesn't matter. She was wearing a pink snowsuit, and she was probably a lot warmer than I was. It was an old car, and the heater wasn't so great. 'Where are we going?' she kept asking me, and I told her to shut her face."

My seatmate stares at me.

"Maybe I hit her, just a light smack," I add without thinking.

She flinches, then busies herself putting up her tray table and wedging her empty plastic glass into the seat pocket in front of her.

"I know her whining was driving me nuts," I explain. "It was hard enough concentrating on the road. Each time I tapped the accelerator, we slid a little to the right. I was steering into the skid like you're supposed to. It was hard to say where the edge of the road was at that point. I was afraid I might drive right off it by mistake."

The green seat belt sign comes on. "We should be landing soon," the woman murmurs. She brushes crumbs off her lap, adjusts her scarf, angles her legs away from me, toward the aisle. We're both still wearing our seat belts.

"Next thing you know, the kid's pulling on the handle to the door, trying to get out."

"So she's in the front seat?" The woman looks like she's reluctant to ask questions, but can't help herself.

"The passenger seat, right next to me. And I'm grabbing at her, and she's saying, 'I'm going to tell my Mommy and Daddy.' I'm getting really pissed off. 'You aren't going to tell your Mommy and Daddy anything,' I say to her, and pull her back by her hair."

The woman looks alarmed, and I decide to wind up. The captain's just announced that we're landing in Burbank in ten minutes and that it's 70 degrees. I'm almost surprised it's not snowing.

"Long story short, I was grabbing at her, we were arguing, the car went into a spin, and we skidded sideways into a telephone pole. It felt like slow motion, but there was nothing I could do. That's what made me think of the angel of death when you said that. My brush with the angel of death."

"What happened? Were you both okay?"

"Right as rain, just shaken up. We walked a mile to a gas station and waited out the storm. Got the car towed, Avis brought a new one, and we were on our way the next morning."

She doesn't look convinced.

I'm still in the scene. Was it an old beater, or was it an Avis rental car? Was it Ohio? It was flat, and a long time ago. I can't remember the last time I was in Ohio for business. I remember getting out of the car and hauling the blonde-haired girl with me, but we weren't walking along the highway to a gas station, we were stumbling in deep snow through a field, walking away from the highway. I was yanking at her arm, and she was bawling. I was cold and wet and afraid somebody was going to see us.

The woman's still looking at me, and I give a reassuring laugh.

"I'm just kidding," I say. "Maybe it was spring, and there was no snow. No little girl. I skidded on an oil slick and hit a telephone pole. Or I would have if I'd gone on a different highway three days later, but I didn't. It could be something I read in the newspaper."

She's already unbuckling her seat belt and hauling an enormous silver bag from under the seat in front of her, leaning with her whole weight on the armrest by the aisle as she stands up. She breathes heavily and adjusts her purple scarf again.

"I hope you have a good trip," I say, extending my arm for a handshake. "What's your name, by the way?"

"Beryl," she says after a moment. She doesn't look me in the eye as we shake hands.

"I'm Herbert," I say, though that's not my name.

My driver's license says Timothy. My wife calls me Tim. I can barely remember what my name was before that.

Something Like That

I don't know why I lied. Maybe it's because someone finally believed me. So maybe it didn't really happen in exactly that way with exactly those boys on exactly that night. I'm not sure anymore. But things have happened to me, on nights like that, with boys like that. I was at a party like that, and a bunch of boys jostled me in the hall on the way to the bathroom. They were laughing and drunk, and I was pinned against the wall and couldn't breathe, and they were reaching under my skirt, clawing at me with their hands in my underpants. I tried to scream, but it was like my throat had closed up and no sound came out. *Lighten up*, one of the guys said when I ran to the front door of the apartment crying. All night I was crying, hiccupping, rocking back and forth like a baby, mascara and snot smeared all over my face. My roommates said, *You got to be careful.* They said I was lucky nothing really happened, not like the girl down the hall who dropped out. And I guess nothing really happened, at least not compared to high school, when I thought I was in love, at least he said he loved me, and then two of his friends showed up when we were making out in the back seat of his car, and they did things to me, and all three of them laughed and called me a slut. Everyone at school was calling me a slut that year. No one cared about my side of the story. In middle school, there were my older cousins who were teaching me how to play pool and kept rubbing up against me from behind when I leaned over the table. *Shame on you*, my mother said. *Don't lie like that. It would break your father's heart if he heard you say things like that about his own brother's boys*. Then there was my other uncle when I was real little, who called me Cutie Pie and always made me sit in his lap. I never told anybody about that, how he tickled me to make me wiggle in his lap and gripped my arms so tight his fingers left marks. So when the reporter was asking girls in my dorm for their stories, maybe I got confused, or maybe it all happened, and it's just hard to remember, because why would I want to remember something like that, or tell a story like that, much less a lie like that?

Hula

He says his name is Philip and he tells you he's from New Jersey, gazing at you intently over a Mai Tai that he slurps through a straw. Mai Tais aren't even Hawaiian, he tells you, they're American, and he asks if you want one, but you've already had three Piña Coladas and you say no thanks, not now. You're feeling a little sick, maybe from the sun on the excursion boat this afternoon, or maybe from the Piña Coladas. He's pasty-faced, no tan at all. Probably just got here today. His lips are wet, a little disgusting really, and you wonder what it would be like to kiss him and whether he has hair on his chest. You don't like too much hair. He's wearing a tight orange polo shirt and smells like cologne. He's buff, probably works out. You feel sort of sick thinking about this stuff and wonder whether you're going back to Philip's hotel with him and hope not but things are a little blurry and maybe you will even though you know it's a bad idea. Let me guess, what are you, twenty-five? I like twenty-five-year-old blondes, he says. Especially if they're all blonde, he adds with a leer, and already you're grossed out, thinking it's loud in the bar, maybe that's not what he said. Philip's got his hand on your shoulder while he's talking to you, and he's leaning too close. His hand slides down and brushes your breast. Whoops, he says, sorry, but he doesn't look sorry, and you know you should leave now but you don't. You here alone, he asks, and you're not, but you're not sure where your girlfriend is and you know she was hoping to get laid tonight. Live a little, she said, it's vacation. So you're letting guys buy you drinks and what is this, a dentist's convention, you can't remember, and you ask Philip, are you here for a dentist's convention or something. Or something, he laughs, and he doesn't explain, and you forget to ask him what he means. There's another Piña Colada in front of you, and you take a gulp, so sweet and cold it makes your teeth hurt. You look around the dark Tiki lounge with plastic plumeria leis and wooden fish on the walls, and really this could be Ohio or anywhere, except everyone's wearing brand new Hawaiian shirts. I have to go to the little girls' room, you say, surprised because that's something your grandmother always said, and he says, why don't we go to my place and you can use mine. I like to hear girls tinkle, you think he says, but you must have misheard him. Why would he like that? As you slide off the bar stool you stagger, which comes as a surprise too, and the room starts to tilt, and he has his hand under your bent elbow to hold you up. Whoops, he says. Steady now. Whoops, you say with an embarrassed laugh. And maybe you'll let him help you get wherever you're going. For a moment you can't remember where that is. What's your name again, he asks, but he's joking with the bartender and handing over some bills and doesn't wait for an answer. I like it doggie style, he says when he turns back to you, so close you can feel his cold saliva and hot breath on your ear, and you don't say anything because that's just gross. Let's hula, baby, he says, pushing you toward the door, one hand still under your elbow, the other gripping your waist, and you're wondering what Hawaiian dancers wear under their grass skirts and whether he wears boxers or briefs, and you hope you're not going to find out, but you're afraid you will. And now you answer his question. My name's Lucy, you say. Lucy. But people are talking loud and howling with laughter and you're not sure he even hears.

My Blue Heaven

Lizbeth

She never liked her name. She was going to change it, once we finished high school. *Molly*'s fine for this town, she said, but I got bigger things in mind. I'm going to try out for one of those music videos, she told me, and she would've made it, she was that pretty. And a great dancer. She was going to be homecoming queen next year. Everybody said so.

Vern

White blonde hair, soft like an angel's. She knew what she was doing, all right. Always flipping it over her shoulders, smoothing it behind her ears, shaking it out, playing with it. Wasn't long before I knowed she was the devil, wrapping my heart in barbed tentacles and squeezing, squeezing. But it was too late then. She had her hooks in me good.

Lizbeth

Course I knew about him. Sugar Daddy Vern. She was my best friend, told me everything. I mean she had a boyfriend at school. Lyle Evans. Everybody knew that. Always at football practice. Then basketball. No after-school job, no money to take her anywhere. She was a girl who liked things, you know, pretty things. I couldn't really blame her. I probably would have done the same, somebody give me all that.

Edna

I talked to Pastor, finally. Watched Vern for months, and then talked to Pastor. At first, I thought it was some daughter thing. We couldn't have children, and there she was, almost twenty years younger than him. But I couldn't close my eyes. He came home late afternoons smelling of her. Slime like shiny snail tracks on his skin. Disgusting. Money started to get short at the end of the month. Pastor said to pray, and I did. I prayed.

Lizbeth

He was sweet in bed, was what she told me. Called her Molly Dolly and sang to her. After, you know. Liked to pretend he was Frank Sinatra crooning with a mike. "Crazy Love." "Are You Lonesome Tonight," he'd sing. "My Blue Heaven." That was another one. Oh, she laughed. "My Blue Heaven."

Vern

Said she wanted to marry me, make babies, but she lied. What are we going to do about your wife, she said, like she cared, but I know for a fact she didn't. She wanted trinkets, makeup, money for the mall, halter tops and too-short shorts and an honest-to-God Victoria's Secret bra. Don't you like it, she said, pushing those pink lace titties in my face, and by God I did. Never talked dirty before her.

Lizbeth
She told me Lyle was sweet and had a real hot body, but he's, you know, young. No ambition. Like I said, she wanted to leave, go places. She was talking about one of those talent shows. *So You Think You Can Dance* or something. Said she might be a studio executive later. It's not like she wasn't smart.

Edna
So finally I talked to him. Vern, I've been praying, I said. Twenty-five years, and it's come to this, you running around with some teenage slut. He didn't say anything at first, but his face got all white. I don't know what to do, he said, and started to cry. It's like the devil got hold of me and won't let go. Oh if it's the devil, I said, then we'll both pray. So we prayed on our knees right then and there.

Motel 6 Clerk
Sure I saw him, but I didn't think nothing of it. It's deer season. Everybody's got a rifle in the gun rack on his pickup. I'm just a clerk. Mr. Viswanathan, he owns the motel, always says, take their money and keep your head down. It's none of your business. I thought maybe he was going hunting. Going to clean the gun first.

Lizbeth
She was going to break it off. That's what she told me. It's not right, she said, him being married and all. But he's so grateful, she said, and always giving me things. It's not like him and his wife are doing it any more. She's too old. So I don't know if she was going to break it off that actual day. But she might've been.

Vern

There weren't no other solution. I prayed the whole way over in the truck, and then I knew. I took the Winchester off the gun rack and opened the motel door. She was sitting on the bed dressed like Jezebel in a see-through red nightie, holding her blonde hair up off her shoulders. Vern, she said, my God what are you doing. I squeezed the trigger. Blast like a motherfucker. The rifle kicked back against my shoulder, me warm all over, one last hard-on for her, and Sweet Jesus, Fuck, it felt so right.

Motel 6 Clerk

Next thing you know there're sirens, cop cars everywhere, red lights spinning, radios crackling. The guy just sat in his truck, waiting for them. You can bet I stayed inside until they had him in cuffs. I called Mr. V., but he didn't want nothing to do with it. You never seen so much blood. And the smell, you don't get that on TV. They pulled out the carpet and repainted, but I don't like to rent out number fourteen. My cousin, he goes to Catawba High, knew that girl. Real pretty, he said. Her name was Molly.

Edna

I don't blame Vern. A girl like that. Pastor says I got to forgive them both, but I know she's burning in hell, and that's the God's truth. I visit him regular, and he prizes that. "You're my angel," he said to me last time. His eyes just as blue as they were back when we were courting. "My little bit of heaven."

The Victim

She swallowed that cherry brandy like it was soda pop, her throat moving up and down as she gulped. I told her to sip, by the way. After, she stuck out her tongue and licked her lips, greedy for more. You couldn't call that girl a victim, not in my book.

I don't care what that woman from the police said. Flashing her badge at my door. "We'd just like to ask some questions," she said, just like on TV.

Well I didn't tell her everything, not by a long shot. I told her the girl was doing some cleaning for me. Sure, she's only twelve years old, but her momma liked the idea of her earning some extra money, babysitting, cleaning, stuff like that. When she was done scrubbing and vacuuming, we sat and talked, and I asked her did she want a shower. She was sweaty; she already told me how she loved my shower stall with them shiny tiles. Nothing like that in her trailer park.

I shown her some pictures before she took her shower, and she was real interested. "I'm prettier than her," she kept saying. "I'm prettier than that one." What I'm trying to say is she knowed she was pretty. She wanted the pictures. When we got to the bottom of the pile and she seen the other ones, she got real quiet. But she knowed she could do those too. I didn't say nothing. I told her I'd pay her for modeling, but I didn't say she had to do nothing. And I never laid a finger on the girl. Don't let her, or that mother of hers, tell you different.

She come out of the shower all rosy, her hair tangled and damp, wrapped in a flowered silk kimono I give her. "Can I keep this?" she asked me. "It's real pretty."

"What would your momma say?" I answered. "Why don't we just keep it here, and you can come over whenever you want to and wear it. That's how the real models do it."

Then I give her the brandy, just to relax her a little, and she starts posing with the kimono slipping off her shoulders. Pouting and preening. A natural. I never told her what to do or nothing. She just knew.

The kimono slipped farther down off her shoulders, and then farther. First you could just see the tops of her child breasts. And then the nipples, soft buds just starting to swell. The light was just right. I took a lot of pictures. Click, click, click. I'm an artist with the camera. Always looking for the perfect girl, the perfect shot.

Finally the kimono slipped off altogether. I didn't tell her to take it off. And I took some more shots. She started moving around, all lazy like. Sitting with her back to me, looking over her shoulder. Lying stretched out on her side. Leaning back on her arms, legs spread. The girl was a natural. I just kept saying, "Beautiful, beautiful," and she kept going.

After, she wanted to see them, so I showed them to her.

"You going to print all these?" she asked.

"Just the best," I said.

"Can I have them?"

"Maybe," I said.

I knew I wasn't going to give them to her. That if she showed them to someone else they might not understand. That's a far cry from saying I did wrong though. I never laid a finger on the girl. She wanted them pictures. She weren't hurt. I didn't sell them or nothing, though I could have. Didn't show them to nobody either.

Let them come back with a warrant. They're not going to find nothing. Nothing.

Let's Play a Game

Are you sitting on cement? Whatever you're leaning against is rough and cold. Opening your eyes seems like too much effort. All of your attention centers on the chill that permeates your body. You retreat into the dark inside your skull.

When you wake again, the first thing you see is the word *SLUT* scrawled in black magic marker on your arm. It doesn't make sense. Why is *SLUT* written on your arm? Your head is throbbing, your mouth dry. Your body aches. Where are you? The cement under you is so cold. You look at the blue dumpster beside you, and then shift your legs, suddenly aware that you're naked, sprawled against a cinderblock wall. You raise your hand to your face. Dried vomit is crusted on your cheek and right shoulder, where someone has written *HA HA*. Who? Your breasts have been circled in black marker like targets. A large arrow points downward, past your navel, to your vagina. Your inner thighs are sticky. Semen? Whose? You begin to shiver, overcome by a wave of nausea, and bend over to throw up a thin trickle of yellow saliva. Where are you? Where are your clothes? You feel a spurt of panic. You pull your knees up to your chest.

You can hardly remember the night before, only bits of it. Two older girls in the dorm invited you to a party, and you were flattered, excited. “Me? You want me to come?” They didn’t ask any of your roommates, just you. You dressed carefully, in tight jeans, black lace-up boots, your favorite pink t-shirt with lace inserts on the shoulders, your faux fur jacket. You looked good, your hair long and shiny, just washed.

The downstairs rooms were noisy when the three of you arrived, hot and packed with people talking, laughing, dancing. You put your jacket on the back of a couch. Is it still there? The music was loud. Some guy gave you a Gatorade with vodka, and then another, and then he disappeared and you were dancing with some other guy who said he was a senior. Broad shoulders, Ben Affleck cleft in his chin. “You’re really cute,” he said, leaning forward to whisper in your ear. He asked you if you wanted to go up to his room for a private drink, but you said no. Didn’t you?

The gray morning light hurts your eyes. Your brain feels like it’s floating in the pale ether above, detached from the leaden weight of your body. You’re in some kind of alley. You can see piles of cardboard boxes and garbage bags brimming with thin ribbons of shredded paper. Your pink t-shirt is draped on one of them, stained and twisted. Your jeans and boots lie on the ground nearby. You don’t see your bra or panties or socks. No jacket. You concentrate on reaching for the t-shirt, but it’s hard to lift your arm, and the t-shirt is too far away.

“Let’s play a game,” he said. Didn’t he say that, handing you a shot glass with something blue in it? “What kind of game?” you asked, flirting. You downed the shot. Maybe another after that? You strain to remember. It was a game. You remember that part.

You shrink back at the sounds of banging and clattering farther down the alley, your heart racing. Should you call for help? Not now.

Not like this. Edging behind the dumpster, you pull your legs in farther, wrapping your arms around them. You fight another surge of nausea and close your eyes to make yourself invisible. Your breathing slows as you drift, enveloped by the dark. You're somewhere else.

"Want to play a game?" You and your older brother played hide-and-go-seek on summer nights back home. You remember huddling behind the neighbor's stone wall, breathless, suppressing your giggles, as he called out, "Kell-eee, Kell-eeee." Bats squeaked as they circled overhead in the lavender twilight. You could smell the honeysuckle on the wall, sweet and sharp. The air was cool on your skin. "Kell-eeeee." His calls grew louder as he came closer, faded as he reversed direction, then grew louder again. Your heart thumped in anticipation as you crouched, ready to flee. Any moment he might round the corner to tag you with a triumphant cry. "You're It!"

Nola

I've tried the internet—"1967 near Arcata, California, missing girl"—with no success. I tried a newspaper search in the online archives of the Humboldt Public Library, scrolling through months of headlines. Train wrecks, storms, mudslides, car accidents, house fires. No missing children. Surely it would have been more than local news.

I asked my mother when I visited her in the nursing home. "Do you remember a girl named Nola? A girl around my age who disappeared?"

She shook her head and turned away. "No, I don't remember anything like that."

But Nola stares at me at night, her face just inches from my own. Elfin and pale, with flaxen hair in untidy tufts and frightened eyes, the milky green of glass marbles. Nola was her nickname, short for what I can't recall. She had a common surname, I think. Jones? Smith?

"I'm sorry, Nola," I want to whisper. "So sorry." But the words won't form themselves.

Fifty years later, fragments of memory have resurfaced in my dreams, vivid and unsettling. The smell of pine needles and wet earth. Dim shafts of light filtered through a dense canopy of branches overhead. Silence broken only by the occasional jeering of a scrub jay or the sudden, agitated twittering of small birds. Gigantic trees towering above us as we hurried home, breathless, our hearts pounding. Only I'm not sure it ever happened.

I remember playing princess for hours with Nola. We'd stand in front of the mirror in the half-light of my parents' bedroom, draped in scarves and my mother's necklaces and bracelets. The room smelled of mothballs and face powder and Shalimar perfume. We dabbed the glass perfume stopper on our wrists, twisted my mother's red lipsticks open and then closed them, afraid we'd get in trouble if we painted our lips.

We had princess names.

"My name's not Cathy," I'd say, "it's Princess Zenobia." I liked four syllables. Esmerelda. Thomasina. Nola liked gemstones. Amber. Topaz. Ruby. "That's not my name," she'd say when I called her Nola. She'd tip her head back, nose in the air. "I'm Princess Sapphire."

We never played at her house, which was like a trailer but on blocks, and with real cement steps. It was on a big lot, dark from the surrounding fir trees. There was a sagging plaid couch in the living room and piles of clothes on the floor, smelling like cigarette smoke. She didn't have a father. Her mother slept a lot—that's mostly what I remember—and we had to tiptoe inside when we went to fetch Nola's diamond tiara and the torn lace dress she liked to wear for our game, an old cocktail dress of her grandmother's.

She was wearing that black lace dress when we tied her to the tree. We were far from the path, deep in the woods. I'm not sure what game we were playing, me and Nola and my school friends Candace and Daria. Hostages maybe. Princess prisoner of war. Nola agreed to play. We didn't make her. We had a clothesline, and we wound it around and around the tree. Her arms were pinned to her sides, and we wound the clothesline around her legs and her arms and her torso and her shoulders and tied it in double knots. There were tears and snot on her face.

"Cathy?" she kept saying. "Please make them stop, Cathy. Don't go, Cathy." She knew the others wouldn't help, but she kept saying my name. "Don't go, Cathy." Her voice was shrill with fear.

Nola should have known that she wasn't my friend when I was playing with Candace and Daria. And besides, we were playing a game. That's what I told myself.

I remember her wails, and how they became fainter as we walked farther, clambering over rocks and shrubs, pushing away small branches that made our eyes tear as they slapped back at us, making our way back to the trail.

Nola never came back, did she?

I can see her mother at our door, her bleached hair a rat's nest, eye makeup smeared, eyes wide with alarm. "Where is Nola?" she kept asking over and over. I hovered in the front hallway, shaking my head. "I don't know," I said. I turned and ran up the stairs.

"Would you please ask your daughter where Nola is."

"She doesn't know," my mother answered. She didn't invite Nola's mother in. She just closed the door.

"Women like her shouldn't have children if they can't keep track of them," my mother said to my father, who put his hand on her arm to keep her from saying more when he saw me leaning over the banister.

I can't remember whether the police visited, or whether I was just afraid the police would visit. We moved away before I started junior high. I never saw Candace or Daria again. I wouldn't know what to say to them even if I could find them after all these years. "Do you remember that day, our game in the woods?" I can imagine their shuttered stares.

I've never told anyone what happened. Or what might have happened, since I really don't know.

It was six months ago, when I was in the city shopping for baby clothes with my daughter, that I thought I saw Nola on the street. Older of course, but with the same pale blonde hair, cut short. The same green eyes. We'd been looking at princess outfits, pink and glittery, so maybe that conjured her apparition. Or maybe it was the fragility of my first grandchild, so tiny and precious, my fears for her future. I haven't been able to stop thinking of Nola since.

I rushed after the woman and put my hand on her shoulder.

"Nola," I said. "Is it you? You're all right?"

She stared at me without recognition.

"I'm sorry," I said. "I didn't mean to do it. You have to believe me. I've always been so sorry."

"I don't know what you mean," she said, pulling away from me. "That's not my name."

"What is your name? Tell me. Sapphire? Ruby?"

She just looked at me, as if I were the one who wasn't all right.

Night after night, my dreams take place in the forest. The still air shimmers with menace. I feel like I've been walking forever, my footsteps muffled by a thick cushion of pine needles. I sense small animals burrowing under the earth, huddled in the roots of trees. I glimpse tiny snakes in the damp leaves, and beetles playing dead, their shells black and iridescent. Sometimes I stop to rest on wet, moss-covered logs, but I don't linger. I'm afraid it will get dark. I'm alone, I'm hurrying, I don't know where. Maybe home to hide behind my mother. Maybe back to Nola, to release her.

I can feel her mounting terror, the clothesline biting into her skin as she struggles. I run faster, through clouds of tiny insects that I brush away from my face, and thickets of twigs that scratch my hands. The woods darken as twilight gathers. I don't know where I am or where the path is. I think I hear Nola's panicked breathing somewhere nearby. I stop and turn in circles, straining to see. The woods begin to whisper. Her face looms in front of me, round and white like the moon behind the trees.

Nola?

Acknowledgments

Profound thanks to Kit Frick, Amy Freels, and Diane Goettel of Black Lawrence Press for their enthusiasm, expertise, and work on this project, and to Raeleen Kao for allowing us to use her wonderful artwork "Inhospitable."

Sincere thanks to the editors of the following literary journals where these stories originally appeared:
Vestal Review, "The Missing Girl"
Tampa Review Online, "You Never Know"
Fjords Review, "Something Like That"
Quarter After Eight, "Hula"
Temenos, "My Blue Heaven" and "The Victim"
Literary Orphans, "Let's Play a Game"
Monkeybicycle, "Nola"

Thank you also to Claire Eder and Kirk Wisland of *Quarter After Eight* for nominating "Hula" for *Best Small Fictions 2017*; to Ross McMeekin for featuring "Nola" in the "Best Short Story I Read in a Lit Mag This Week" series on the *Ploughshares* blog; and to J.T.

Hill and the editors of *Monkeybicycle* for nominating "Nola" for a Pushcart Prize and for *Best of the Net 2016*.

Thank you to my San Francisco writing group, the Leporine Conspiracy, especially Alia Volz, for their invaluable advice and support.

And thank you to Steve and Ben, for everything.

Photo: Monica Michelle

Jacqueline Doyle's flash has appeared or will soon appear in *Hotel Amerika, Quarter After Eight, PANK, Monkeybicycle, Sweet, The Café Irreal, Post Road, The Pinch,* and the anthology *Nothing to Declare: A Guide to the Flash Sequence.* She has published short stories and essays in the *Gettysburg Review, Southern Humanities Review, Catamaran Literary Reader, Superstition Review, Confrontation, South Dakota Review, Phoebe,* and elsewhere. Her work has earned Pushcart nominations, Best of the Net nominations, and Notable Essay citations in *Best American Essays.* She lives with her husband and son in the San Francisco Bay Area, where she is a professor of English at California State University, East Bay.